Wilhem

By
Chloe Brogan

Trigger Warning

Mentions of abandonment, physical abuse, stabbing, neglect, nightmares, mental illness, paranoia, murder, blood and gore, violent and disturbing language, dismemberment and animal dismemberment, prostitution, and mentions of violent sexual encounters.

Dear Roman,

I hope this correspondence finds you well. I've been praying for you on your travels. Mother suggested that I write to you now since you left. Sadly, my penmanship is still not ideal. Mother says I need imr improvement so I should hand write to you, but honestly, I think I will find work so I can afford a type-writer. I would borrow Dad's, but since Mother ran him out I'm not sure where to find his things. Mother took his stuff and burned it. She dragged his suits, his uniform, the flag, and all the photos we had. It was devastating, but I'm sure you aren't surprised. Only we know what Mother is like when she's angry. She wanted me to lie to you. I'm sure that's no surprise as well. As the Bible says, "You shall not give false witness against your neighbor." Or brother, in this case.

I searched in the ashes from the fire pit. Not much I could save, unfortunately. I saved his silver cuff flinks, with the little hummingbird etched into them, the ones you liked so much. Do you have any idea where Dad's typewriter is? I looked in Mother's shed for his other things. She still hasn't changed the combination lock from Rody's birthday. Of course, she uses our little brother's

birthday. She must become more clever or at least make it less obvious he's the favorite. If he wasn't so vile, I would sit back and accept his coat of many colors. I found her wedding dress; it was pristine. I can't imagine her ever fitting into the small cream dress or why she keeps it. She never had girls, but I guess if it's hers she could never part with it.

How is New York City? I pray you found work quickly. Mother will ask you for money. I recm recommend not sending it or she will expect a monthly "gift". Remember when I worked that summer delivering milk? It took me twice as long to save any money.

I am considering a move myself, but not as far. I won't be able to sneak off like you did. She is more cautious now. I also can't disrespect her wishes for me to stay near. I do not want a ticket to Hell. Cincinnati is much closer to Batavia and she will find it more agreeable. Mother loves shopping there. Doc Martin also told mother that the economy is doing much better and Cincinnati has been bustling.

Speaking of Doc Martin, he has been around a lot. He has aged quite a bit since we were children. His glasses are thicker than coke bottles. He barely comes to my shoulder, Roman. His hair is no longer black with a white skunk stripe but the reverse. He still breathes through his mouth like an invalid, though. I have heard far too much between him and Mother. That woman is so crude, talking about our dad and her husband like he is dead. Parading around with Doc like he left years ago, not only a month. It takes every ounce of my strength not to slug him when he looks at me and says; "Oh Willy, son, I'm here for you and your brothers. Think of me as your dad, hell, call me Dad." He could be our damn grandfather. I know he means well, but it stirs such a rage in me.

I wish you were here, Roman. You helped make being stuck in this good-for-nothing house not be quite as terrible. You are such a blessing in my life. Now that you're gone, I feel your absence most when I have to deal with Mother alone.. She hates me. I miss your ability to soften her blows and bring levity to situations. She spends all her time telling everyone that the only reason she ended up with dad was because of me. The only good thing that came from dad was you and "Rody". She's been doting on him more now that dad's gone, but at least that means she is not yelling at me.

Mother says I have no potential. I can't argue with her, though. There is nothing I love to do, and nothing I am skilled at. God has not presented me with an obvious gift. Maybe I can find something I like in Cincinnati. Possibly meet some girls. Mother told her sewing group that I can't talk to women and if she ever hoped for grandkids from me, she'd have to arrange a marriage. It was mortifying. I was right there. Nancy Remel told her I was handsome and Mother laughed. Mother said I look too much like father and didn't have the charm to match.

Mother mocks me when she's laying bricks with a disgusting seventy-year-old. I bet with how he damn well throws money at her, his dangler barely fucking works.

I think I may be able to convince

Doc to let me borrow his black Buick Brewster to find work in Cincinnati on the last Sunday, which is probably when you'll receive this. He keeps offering me an office assistant's job at his office. I heard the rumors about his last assistant and how his wife left because of her. Mother would just hate me more if I stole Doc away from her. I do look better in a pencil skirt than her, though.

What else have you missed? Mother makes Rody sleep with her now Dad is gone. I won't get into how strange that is right now. So the room is all mine. It makes it hard to sort out my thoughts, no one to talk to except myself. I can't sleep either.

The nightmares are worse now that you can't wake me from them. The most recent one that keeps playing in my mind is the worst. My dreams scare Rody still. He acts brave like I'm telling him a ghost story, but I can't risk him telling Mother of them now. My nightmares used to be of a big bad wolf chasing me. Now it's something else chasing me. I hesitate to share the dream with you, but you've been the only one who's ever understood them and helped ease my mind.

I went to bed two nights ago. I could barely sleep with Mother having a blanket party with Doc. Rody was asleep on the couch with the radio on as loud as possible. So I got soused.

Luckily I had bought some scotch. Looking back, I'm sure it didn't help my thoughts wandering around the eerie dark hallways of that old brick house. Every creek in the floors felt like someone calling my name. Roman, it felt like those hideous red walls were closing in on me. My heart began to race. I kept telling myself it wasn't real. Then there was a deep low animalistic breathing. A snarl not like a wolf. My feet froze, I wondered if I should play dead or run. I looked over my shoulder and all I saw was darkness. But then the darkness moved. I may be twenty-one but I have never sprinted to our room so quickly.

I climbed into my bed. My chest

was so tight that I could barely breathe. I sat and finished the whole damn bottle. I laid my head down and covered it like a damn child. It was mortifying. Finally, the drink took me and I faded off to sleep. Roman, when I fell asleep, I woke up from my dream. I need to leave here. I think that's why the dreams are getting worse. Please don't let Mother know the dreams are back. Please pray for me.

Blessings,

Willie

C. E. Brogan

Dear Roman,

I'm sorry you haven't found work yet. At least you aren't trapped here. I'm glad you found a woman who is willing to deal with you. I know I wouldn't! Just teasing, brother. You were always the handsome one, no matter what Mother says. I'm sure you've put on some muscle walking and hitchhiking all the way to New York.

How is New York really, though? Mother tells me it's dangerous, whereas Doc says it's stunning. You said you can walk to most places, so at least you don't have to try to buy a car. I hate having to all be crammed into a tiny car just to get some eggs and bread.

Mother is trying to set me up with a spinster ten years my senior and fatter than herself. I can't imagine ever having children with her. 31 is too old to be bearing children. Doc agreed with me. He's been frustratingly a God send.

Mother, Rody, and Doc are such a "perfect" little family. I'm sure she is waiting with bated breath to have me leave so she can pretend I don't exist. If I even mention you or dad, Mother throws a fit--throwing plates and screaming. I think that's why

she agreed for me to find work in
Cincinnati. Far enough to keep me
out of her mind, but close ###
enough to control. At least that's
what she thinks.

God has sent me a reprieve in
Doc, though. Doc has made things
more peaceful. He's kind enough.
Given his age and career, though,
I can tell Mother picked him for
his wealth. But Doc keeps Mother
and Rody busy and he lets me
borrow his black Buick. The car
smells like he smokes cigars one
right after the other on his way
home from his office. He isn't
very tidy either.

Doc leaves things randomly
throughout the house and it's
pissing me off. I have tripped on

his briefcase more than once. So,
in a fit of frustration, I threw
it out his Buick window while
driving. I felt awfully guilty,
but it was quite comical to watch
the old egg searching for it. He
just assumed he lost it, instead
of someone else absconding with
it, which I think is commendable
in some ways.

Speaking of which, I took Doc's
Buick to Cincinnati. I applied for
a few jobs. There are a few places
I'm interested in, and a few I'm
not so interested in. I applied
to the post office. They have
pensions, and a government job is
as close as I'll get to being in
the military. God gave me these
damn flat, webbed feet. Mother
always said that I had built in

flippers. Maybe I should try out
for the Olympics. That would be a
gas!

  You asked me, so I asked Mother.
I'm sorry but no, Mother says
she doesn't know nor care where
Dad has gone. I have asked a few
times. Every day I get the mail,
so I know he still hasn't written.
Dad may contact you, please let
me know if he does. Tell him
I'm praying for him. I know he
would've taken me if he could've.
Sometimes I think maybe-if I could
get a letter to him-he'd let me
join him wherever he's gone. But,
maybe God has other plans for
me. It's always hard to know. I
plan on sending a letter to Aunt
Millie to see if he's with her in
Kentucky.

I wanted to thank you! The typewriter was right where you said it was. I found a few more things in the attic. Mother must not know about this stuff. God is good because I found a colt police revolver. It's in stunning condition. I remember Mother being fiercely against them since that's how her mother killed herself. When I held it in my hands, I thought of her, and what it must feel like to take your own life or the life of another. The cool metal rested heavily in my hand, and I wondered if I could conjure a gun like that in my dreams. I wonder if I would be granted relief if I slayed the beast in my nightmares.

Dad took good care of it. Why

wouldn't he have taken it? I also found a book on taxidermy. I heard that it can #be quite a lucrative hobby. I might try my hand at it. Remember when I dissected that cat? I'm sure it can't be so different from that.

Don't worry I will keep the gun safe. We can't discuss it further. I don't want Mother to take any of these letters and learn about it.

I've caught some glimpses of Mother happy, now that Doc is here. Almost on a daily basis, she is distracted by him. So I can hide them instead of tossing them out. I saw her digging through the trash after you returned my correspondence. Filthy woman.

Mother makes me so angry. I know
you must hate living on a friend's
couch but it must be better than
living with her. I feel trapped
and alone in a house full of
people who despise me. She scolded
me yesterday for not being more
like Rody. I wanted to strangle
her but I couldn't, God is testing
my patience not my strength.

Maybe I'm still hoping she'll
love me again.

Mother has given Rody so much
freedom that you and I never got.
He comes and goes as he pleases.
I'm sure if Mother knew that Mrs.
Lester's new baby wasn't her
husband's; she wouldn't like her
sweet innocent Rody as much. He's
a fucking wet sock. If I were to

say anything less than praise
about Rody I'd get the belt. He'll
rat me out for anything. He even
told Mother I was walking around
getting drunk at night. Bitch hid
all the booze for herself.

I bought more, but she found
it and took it as well. The
nightmares won't stop now. I
pray for the Lord to take them,
but maybe the dreams are a test.
I can't sleep at all in fear
of whatever beast lurks on the
other side of counting sheep. My
nightmares are becoming hauntingly
realistic.

Yesterday I was sitting with Rody
on that disgusting green couch
listening to a rugby match during
a hard storm last week. It was

only a quarter after four. The sky
made it seem like midnight. Then,
the power went out. Rody was too
freaked out to go replace the fuse
and Mother was out with Doc.

  Rody wouldn't stop crying.
Sixteen and still afraid of the
dark. It's shameful if I'm honest.
So I stand up and negotiate my
way to the basement door in the
kitchen. The floorboards creaked
so loud I felt it in my brain.
Once I reached the doorknob, my
hand turned to ice.

  I could feel it. The beast
breathing down my neck, the chill
ran down my spine. Each moist
breath timed with mine perfectly.
I'd breathe in and the beast would
breathe out. The smell made my

stomach lurch. The beast smelled of putrid remains. It took every bit of will I had to turn that handle. I swung the door open and ran through-slamming the door behind me.

It made Rody scream, which made it worth it.

The moist, mildewy air of the basement smelled like the beast. It was almost as if instead of entering the basement, I entered the mouth of the beast. I think it was just my imagination, but when I touched the wall, my hand pressed into flesh. It was damp and soft. I pushed on.

The stairs felt odd as I descended, almost as if they were

slick with mud, and I caught
myself sliding with each step.
I made it down to the fuse box.
Luckily a flashlight was still
in it from Dad. I turned on the
flashlight and began to replace
the fuse. Then I heard it; the
door creaked. Then the sounds of
cloven hoofs raced down the steps.
I swear the devil himself was
running down those rickety wooden
stairs.

I heard a snarl at the bottom.
I hit the fuse, and the basement
illuminated. But nothing was
there. NOTHING ROMAN! The steps
weren't wet; the walls were dryer
than bones! Either I've lost it or
the house is haunted. No matter
which it is, I need to get out of
here.

Please write soon. These letters
are all I look forward to here.

Blessings,

Willie

C. E. Brogan

Dear Roman,

I'm glad you finally found work.
I do worry you may be rushing
things with this woman you met.
Remember, puppy love only lasts
so long. Mother played games with
Dad as well and we saw that turned
out. The Lesters, for example,
have been married for twenty years
at least, and now the Misses has
birthed a babe that little Rody
Fathered.

I'm not sure any woman is truly
"good". Yes, I know we are all
born evil, but I think for women
it's harder to become good. Like

Eve, all women are inherently manipulative and look to go against man's rules and God's rules. I have never met a woman who doesn't have some disgusting secret or horrible natural flaw. I just implore you to make a wise choice instead of jumping head-first into the shallow end.

I interviewed with a woman at the post office. I didn't get the job. I couldn't imagine taking directives from the bitch who interviewed me. She had her hair and makeup all done up like she was going to a show. FOR WORK! She had a wedding ring, and she was parading around at the post office with all these innocent men— tempting them. I could never work with a woman with such callous disregard for others.

  After that interview, I
interviewed for a butcher shop.
The owner, Marcus Wilkins, liked
me. Few seem to understand my dry
humor, but he did. He also has
no wife or children to distract
him from work. I admire a man
with such drive and focus. I do
find his grizzled gray beard
unsanitary. Imagine if any of his
beard hair fell into ground beef.
HORRIFYING. DISGUSTING.

  He also offered me a place to
stay at his small farm right
outside the city. I could ride
into the shop with him during the
weekdays and make a little extra
as a farm-hand on the weekends.

I could be free of Mother and the new replacement family she has created with Doc and Rody. I feel like an outsider in the home I was born in. It's infuriating and my heart breaks knowing I was never wanted there. Mother shockingly is all for this position. I'm sure part of her is happy. She has never liked me. But she would lose the grasp she has around my life.

Marcus also is going to train me all himself. He says he has a feeling I have potential. A first since most people see me as a hindrance. I know sometimes you feel that way about me, too. I understand it can be difficult dealing with me. No matter how I try, I struggle to conform into this family. Possibly because of how "unnecessarily" honest I am. Proverbs 12:22. I have always felt that God gave me my honesty; that I am a vessel of truth. I do know, however, that it can sometimes make it harder to love me.

At least I'll have somewhere to fit in. Hopefully.

I am nervous though. I may have dissected a few stray cats but never something as large as a pig or cow. Possibly I should practice on Mother? I'm just pulling your leg. I know we jest about it but she has been pushing things lately. Like the sudden aversion to alcohol. She would make wine in the basement for her friends while it was still against the law. I'm sure Doc has something to do with it. He always tells Mother it's not good for her liver. He never seems concerned about my liver, though. Maybe he knows I'll be a lost cause.

It's frustrating here without you. Everywhere I go people are morons. In this house, I have more intellectual conversations with the rats in the wall than the people who claim to be family. I miss when you and Dad were here, it appears you two were the only people I could hold a conversation with. Everyone else is stupid or plainly exasperating. I am hoping my new boss is like you and Dad. It would be a blessing to have a man in my life that could guide me and fill me with fulfilling conversation.

Remember when Dad would take us three boys to the park and talk about philosophy? We'd go to the park, and he'd tell us about Socrates and Plato. There was one morning when he taught us about St. Augustine of Hippo. How his philosophy of "If I'm mistaken, I am" was turned into "I think, therefore I am" by Descartes. I remember that day so well. We three boys just sitting eating sandwiches and getting sunburned.

I digress. I have a new one for you to ponder. Does gender affect your morals? I have found that women do not have the same consciousness as men. While a man would never steal unless necessary, like feeding his family. I've noticed that a woman

may easily be tempted by earrings
and follow her innate nature of
evil.

 Or possibly, do men have stronger
will power than women? I find
Mother and other women will be
h####hysterical and let their
inner rages release more than
men. Men are expected to be fully
composed in all situations, but
women are allowed to make utter
fools of themselves.

 In that question, I pose another.
Is there truly good or evil? Or
is that society trying to label
opportunities for people to fight
their innate animal instincts of
hunting and conquering? Are there
good guys or bad guys? Is it just
the winners of societal standards

that determine what is good?

I have read of conflicts going on between Germany and the surrounding nations. I'm sure if England was to win, they would tell of the evil Germans just as they did for the Great War. Now if the Germans were to win, the world would deem them heroes instead.

As you can tell, I have been pondering on the topics of good and evil. I'm sure you are wondering, "what has brought up all of my dear brothers' thoughts on good and evil?" Well, Roman, I have been having those nightmares nightly since Mother poured out all the drink I had.

I have come to the conclusion

that my nightmares may actually
be dreams. Like Daniel in the old
testament. For warnings. I am
hoping by the time you receive
this I will be out of this house
and can find freedom or possibly
reprieve from these dreams.

Blessings,

Willie

Dear Roman,

Love is such a strong word. The Oxford dictionary defines the word love to mean an intense feeling of deep affection. It doesn't mean long-term. I only say this as a concerned older brother. I may have never been the c##charismatic Casanova you were with women. But I worry you may rush things. Does this 'Mags' know about our family? The things we've been through? I would assume most women would be faint at the harsh parenting we received. Or the way we acted out. I just ask you to reflect on whether you truly love

"Mags" and whether this intense feeling is long-term for BOTH of you. If so, I am truly happy for you.

You said you started working for some delivery businesses. I know it's not your dream but providing is more important. Especially if you want to provide for Mags. I also think physically demanding jobs are good for you. It strains the body but gives your mind time to think freely.

I hope you can find joy in my own recent accomplishment. I am officially apprenticing under Marcus Wilkins for Wilkins Butchers. I am excited about this opportunity. He has to clear the room in his farmhouse before I can move in. Luckily Doc Martin is allowing me to use his Brewster for the first week of work. After that, hopefully, I will be at Wilkins Farm or I will have to figure out my own transportation.

  I went to my first day, yesterday. I had to leave at dawn or I wouldn't have made it in time. I also arrived a touch early so I was able to admire the streets of Cincinnati. It's quite a bustling city, but also filthy. The Wilkins Butchershop is near the distasteful section of Cincinnati. Two streets over from drugs, pimps, and disgusting streetwalkers. I am not fond of the location. I guess I will have to become accustomed to it.

Marcus says it's a perfect location. Right by the rich neighborhoods and only a few streets off from the unsavory part of the city. Marcus says that he keeps prices right in the middle of cheap and expensive. So the rich come for what they consider a steal, and the poor come on paycheck day to get nicer meat than what they are used to.

Marcus showed me how to use the meat grinder. There is something relaxing about putting chunks of flesh in a grinder and it coming out as one mass. As if the meat is being reassembled in a new form. It's still the same meat, but somehow it seems completely different. I couldn't help but pick it up and feel the wet, slimy mass of ground meat slide through my fingers. I joked to Marcus that it must be what the brain felt like, and he told me he would butcher a pig tomorrow and show me what a brain felt like. I was half tempted to squeal like a schoolgirl being asked to a dance.

I have never met someone who has ENCOURAGED my unique curiosity. After he showed me the grinder, he took me to the meat cold room. Marcus swung open the hefty metal door to the darkroom. Before I even stepped through. The cold felt like an icy night in the dead of winter. Once I breathed in, my lungs froze. If I'm honest, my nipples felt like they could cut diamonds.

When I tell you the sight I
saw. It stirred something in
me. Animals hanging from hooks.
Pigs, cows, ducks, and chickens.
All on display, like a work of
art in a gallery. I know it's
disturbing for most, but they
were all perfectly aligned. All
exposed to show their truth. What
lies beneath the skin after death?
Nothing. No soul, no judgment,
just flesh.

It's almost refreshing. Death
is looked upon as a distasteful
thing. Remember, at Nan's funeral
where Mother wept and wept? The
week before, she was saying she
couldn't wait for her inheritance.
That freezer showed me so much.
Life is a lie, and only death can
bring the truth out. Death is a

gift from God, truly.

You should take note of that.
Life is a lie,' and only death can
bring truth.

Doc is allowing me to use the
Buick to drive back and forth
until I can take my things to
Marcus's abode.

I must tell you, my dreams
are becoming more tolerable.
Last night I dreamt something
horrifying, yet it has brought me
some peace.

I went to bed at my usual
hour. I got my hands on Mrs.
Lester's vodka. When we talked, I
insinuated I knew of her and Rody.
I implied if she didn't want Mr.
Lester knew she should help me.

I took a few shots and stuffed
the bottle in the wardrobe. I was
hoping for a dreamless night.
Instead, the beast returned.

I could hear it scratching at my
door. Snarling and snorting for
my scent. I felt cold. Not fear,
just cold emptiness. I attempted
to move, but I was stuck. The
comforter on me weighed me down,
binding me to the bed. I couldn't
even sit up to look. All I could
hear was the cloven hooves pacing.
I shut my eyes tight.

The smell was sickly sweet, as if
the beast had eaten rotten meat.
It was pungent, but I didn't feel
ill. I felt my skin tighten when I
heard Mother. Her hefty footsteps
walking the wooden floor. Mother

creaks the loudest with her walk,
punishing the poor floors for her
overconsumption.

That's when I became fearful.
What if she saw me cowering from
a horrible dream? I was sure
she would beat me and spout
profanities. Then I heard the
beast stop. No more scraping off
the door. No more snarls, just
silence.

Then I heard its cloven hooves
charge. I could hear Mother's
screams. It was almost euphoric
hearing her suffer. It made all
the hair on my body stand on end.
The gnashing and screams felt
like revenge. I finally gained
the strength to sit up as silence
fell. I heard dragging. Possibly

the beast was dragging Mother
somewhere. I looked at the bottom
of the door and blood seeped
underneath. The beast scratched
at the door once more. A reminder
that it was still there. The beast
seemed as if it was satisfied
though, and let me drift off to
sleep.

Don't think of me as cruel. I
have no control over my dreams.
How many times did she whip us
till we were raw and screaming? I
know we spoke of doing monstrous
things to pay her back in kind.
This will be the closest I will
ever get to that. I could sleep,
though. Sleep hard and wake up
fully refreshed for the first time
in months. Possibly the best sleep
I have ever experienced.

Rody actually had to wake me in the morning when I am always the first to rise. You know I've always been an insomniac. I think my life is finally on the right track. Soon enough, I will be on my own. Twenty-three may seem old to get my life together, but I'm proud.

I hope you are proud of me, too.

Blessings,

Willie

P.S. Have you heard from Dad?

C. E. Brogan

Dear Roman,

I appreciate your concern. I have no interest at the moment to seek out a Doctor for these dreams. You know my thoughts on medication. Nor I do not wish to become an empty-headed lobotomy experiment just for better sleep.

I have had dreams for years. You know this. They may be a burden, but one I'm willing to carry.

I am glad to hear you finally have your own place. I worry that you have done this with Mags. It seems you are moving very quickly

with someone you barely know. What
could she be keeping from you?
Could she be tricking you? The
repercussions could be devastating
to your heart. You are an adult,
though, and must make mistakes on
your own.

I'm disappointed to hear he
hasn't reached out yet. I wrote
to his sister in Kentucky. She
still has not responded. Marcus
also allowed me to post a missing
poster in his butcher shop. I just
want to know dad is okay, I'm sure
you do as well.

Speaking of Marcus; he fixed up
his barn loft to be a small loft.
No plumbing yet. He said he would
teach me how to run electricity
and plumbing. It's pretty empty.

At least Mother allowed me to take the old mahogany wardrobe and my bed. The only other thing she allowed me to take was my clothes. She gave our radio to Rody. She also gave him my model trains and airplanes. Since she has decided that the only things I have left of dad is "childish" and should go to her "little angel Rody". Those are the only things in there at the moment. I snuck Father's gun with me. I am living just on the outskirts of Cincinnati. It can be dangerous.

I've realized recently the sheer volume of unsavory people I come in contact with; I'm not sure if Marcus even realizes the amount of scum surrounding us. Normally when Marcus locks up the butcher shop we exit out the back to the alleyway. He parks his truck back there, so we have more room for patrons to park in the front. Then last night, a whore approached us. She was missing her front two teeth, her hair was bright red, and she was wearing a black flapper dress. The kind that swishes as a woman walks and lands above her knee-which were scuffed.

She introduced herself as Candy and asked if we were builders looking to lay some bricks. Candy winked at me and said, "New meat, Marky? He looks like a virgin." She laughed and grabbed my hand. "I could help with that." I ripped away my hand after she winked at me. It took every ounce of my will not to scream at the woman. She and Marcus exchanged some words, but I was too red hot with anger. To think this pro-skirt has any right to utter a word to Marcus after insulting me.

"Oh, Candy, your name sticks true. You are too sweet to offer to this young man." Marcus just smiled and waved her off.

Candy then walked past me and kissed me on the cheek. I almost vomited. I took a shower back at the farm. Trying to scald her sin off my skin. I couldn't help but think about if I had taken her up on her offer while in the shower. I will spare you the details.

I've never been with a woman in that way. Mother browbeating us that it was sinful has made that thought not cross my mind. Of course, I also don't want to end up having children with someone who is not perfect. Our mother tainted dad's pedigree.

Dad told me about how Mother knew his fascination with eugenics and lied about her lineage. She had told him she was English when in reality her father was a Mick. Her Irish blood shows in her anger and now Rody has had a bastard child. It's a perfect example of how your lineage can not only affect your physical body but your morals as well. We must do better. We must find women who will repair what was broken.

Tell me more about Mags? Have

you asked her about her family
history? I am guessing since you
had said she is a blonde and
blue-eyed "doll" she has nordic
descent? From what I read, people
of Nordic descent are quite hardy.
She sounds quite kind as well.
I still have my doubts since
we haven't been acquainted yet.
Possibly with working, I can
afford to visit you in New York
City. Meet this young woman.

Breeding is a topic that's been
on my mind a bit. It was spurred
on by Marcus asking if I'd like to
raise some pigs. I already live
in the barn and the chickens just
roam the property so the ground
floor is open for animals. He said
if I did, he'd pay me for them if
they were fine enough to butcher.

Pork sells well around here.
Marcus has multiple farms he works
with but says it'd be nice to have
a few from birth to butcher. He
says it's more meaningful. Then
it's not some stranger killing
them but a person who loves them
and can put them to rest. He's a
good man.

I haven't gotten to butcher
anything myself yet. I mostly work
at the counter. The regulars tease
me and call me stiff. I'm not sure
what to do. I am very friendly,
I'm just not charismatic like you,
Roman. It makes me angry. I wish
I could just be like you and Dad.
Handsome and funny. My spindly
body and weak chin I could pass
for a teenage boy. The boyish
blonde and blue eyes certainly

don't help. I'd much rather be
in the back away from all the
unnecessary pleasantries that I
just can't seem to master.

I got to watch Marcus butcher the
front quarter of a beef cow. This
animal is so monstrously large.
Yet Marcus took apart the cow with
such elegance. We walked into
the cold room and there was half
a beef cow hung along with the
other meat like ornaments. You'd
never know it was a cow, its hide
was gone along with its head and
hoofs. The scarlet of its flesh
marbled with beautiful white fat.

Marcus took his butcher knife
and showed me to cut between the
twelfth and thirteenth rip. He
took his butcher knife, and it

slid through the cold flesh like a hot knife in butter. Only stopping at the vertebrae of the bovine. He then handed me the handsaw to cut through the spine. The crunch of the vertebrae bone underneath the dull handsaw sent shivers down my spine. Moving it back and forth almost sounded like a zipper of a pair of trousers was continually unzipped.

I can understand now why Marcus is so fit for forty. I couldn't get all the way through, so Marcus finished. Watching his strong arms and well-built muscles slice through bone was… Different. It makes me want to gain that level of strength. Become stronger and a finer specimen. I have come to appreciate everything about Marcus in the last few months that I've been here. His calm attitude, and the way he conducts himself around the regulars, is something I can only hope to emulate someday. I watch him constantly, finding every opportunity to be as near to him as I can be. He makes me feel like I'm capable of more than I ever expected of myself. I have even considered growing a beard recently. I never would have tried before, but Marcus promises it would help shape my face better. I believe him. You and Dad always had that strong muscular build with little to no effort. I will obviously need to put some effort in so if you have any recommendations. I will happily take them.

Blessings,

Willie

P.S. I am not being vain, I just
want to become… stronger.

Dear Roman,

The more I hear about this, Mags,
the more she sounds like a good
fit for you. I do worry about
how she will contribute to you.
Will she support you to become a
thriving, smart man of society?
Will she bear many children to
pass on the family name? I'm
glad you have moved up to a more
managerial position. You have
wonderful leadership skills.

Does this business have a
pension? I don't know how much
you have heard about the war in
Europe. I find the whole situation

fascinating. A nobody turned into
a somebody overnight. I would love
to hear what you've heard. I'm
sure you have more accurate press
than the Cincinnati Enquirer.

I know you think I should speak
kinder of Mother, even though you
agree she is an unnecessarily
cruel person. This is between us.
I feel like I should be allowed
to express my disdain. I think if
you understood what she's done to
Dad. Emasculating him in front
of his children. I can't help
but replay the night he left in
my head no matter what I try. Is
there anything I could've done?
Would he have taken me with him
if I had spoken up? It's been a
few months now, yet it sits in my
mind like yesterday. You weren't

there; I wish you had been, so we could commiserate. I think writing it out will help ease my troubled mind and will explain how our mother is truly a vile human.

It was after Easter dinner. The evening was cold; nevertheless, an ominous forewarning, I believe. My blood boils thinking about it.

Just as Dad normally did, dad took us boys to pick out a ham from the butcher. Rody was rude and dull going on and on about Mrs. Lester the whole ride. How attractive she is, how good her candies are, and how sweet she is. Which are fine qualities, but the woman is short a few screws and is a converted heeb. Dad and I sat quietly listening to him droning on. I much preferred when you rode along. Instead of women, we would talk philosophy as the bumbling moron, Rody, would twiddle his thumbs.

Anyways, we picked up a ham and got back in Dad's Ford sedan. Rody the idiot started in on Mr. Lester, which, as you know, is Dad's dearest friend. Rody just absolutely ignored the clear uncomfortability in Dad's face. I was in the back seat and I could see the anger seeping out. Rody said Mr. Lester was an ugly little man, Dad just sat through it. You know how Mother is if anyone tells her precious Rody to stop.

Then Rody said the one thing that pisses Dad off. Which, as

you know, is attacking someone's character. It happened in almost slow motion for me. Rody says in a snarl, "That weak little selfish man could never please Mrs. Lester…" I saw Dad's hand raise and then heard the crack of his hand connecting Rody's face.

"How fucking dare you!" Rody hissed at our Dad. Dad pulled over the car; his face was crimson with rage.

"Now listen here, you rotten boy. Your mother has ruined you. I can't believe you are my child. Some days, I wish you weren't. You're a part of the problem with this world. You will leave your Mother's home someday and be NOTHING with that damn attitude. I could raise your brother better. I allowed your Mother to coddle you and you have rotted in intellect and soul. If someone is weak and selfish, it's you, boy. I pray you never have children because they will be the blight of this damn world. Now get your ass in the back seat Rodney I can't stand looking at your ugly mug. Willie, come sit up here."

Rody went to rebuttal and Dad slapped him again. "It's too late, boy. Tell your Mother if you wish I no longer care what that pig of a woman thinks if she raised a monstrosity like you." I have never seen Dad that angry before. Rody didn't hesitate to switch seats with me.

The rest of the ride was quiet. Dad was gripping the steering wheel, his knuckles white. I dare not speak, but I didn't want to either. The silence was relaxing besides Rody's insistent muttering in the back seat. Pouting like a young child with his arms crossed.

We pulled into the drive of the house, the off blue it is painted looked less welcoming and more like the sky before the storm. Rody jumped out of the car to run inside. Dad looked at me solemnly. I will never forget what he said to me.

"William, I am sorry I didn't show you to be a man. I have been jealous of Roman. Going off, leaving the monster that is your

mother and yet you're still here because you are just like me. It wasn't right that your mother pulled you from university lying, saying I was sick and she needed your help. Of all our boys, you are the smartest and could become something fantastic. We need to get out of here, son. I am sorry you inherited my cowardice."
He left the car before I could respond.

I should've stopped him. I should've told him to just back out of the drive and we would run. What if I had? What if we could've joined you?

Once I entered the house, the chaos had already begun.

Mother screamed, "YOU WORTHLESS MAN HOW DARE YOU RAISE A HAND TO MY SON!" She started towards Dad with a paring knife.

"He is OUR son and YOU'VE RUINED HIM." Dad hissed.

"I WILL KILL YOU ROBERT! HOW DARE YOU! YOU ARE NOTHING COMPARED TO MY RODY." Rody was standing behind Mother with a shit-eating grin sprawled across his face.

Dad walked away from her just as he normally does. Then Mother revealed a dark truth.

"HE'S NOT EVEN YOURS YOU HIDEOUS LITTLE MAN. YOU ARE NOTHING TO ME OR HIM. YOU THINK YOU'RE SO DAMN SMART WITH YOUR DAMN DEGREE. YOU ARE NOTHING. A FILTHY MAN WHO

CAN'T PLEASE ANYONE. YOUR LUCKY
I ALLOWED YOU TO COME NEAR ME TO
PRODUCE THOSE WEAKLINGS. ROMAN
WILL DO NOTHING WITH HIS LIFE
AND NEITHER WILL WILLIAM. YOU PUT
THEIR NOSES INTO BOOKS INSTEAD
OF GIVING THEM STRENGTH. THEY
ARE HIDEOUS LIKE YOU, TOO." She
then paused, searching for Dad's
reactions.

Dad smirked, "Thank God for he
is good and that vile creature is
not my spawn." He turned away and
started down the hallway, Mother
followed him and threw the paring
knife at him. It sunk into his
right shoulder and he fell to his
knees.

Mother began crying and
screaming, "I WANT YOU TO

APOLOGIZE YOU FILTHY OLD MAN! YOU ARE NOTHING COMPARED TO RODNEY! YOU WILL BE QUIET THE REST OF THE DAY AND MAKE EASTER DINNER!"

Dad stood up and pulled the knife out of his shoulder. Still smiling, he looked back at Mother, "I don't believe I will make Easter dinner or any more dinners." The blood ran down the back of his shirt as he continued into his room next to Mothers.

Mother looked at me and said, "IF YOU DON'T WANT TO BE NEXT GO TO YOUR DAMN ROOM YOU DISGUSTING BOY! YOU ARE JUST AS MUCH AS A DISAPPOINTMENT AS YOUR FATHER, WHO LIVES WITH THEIR MOTHER AT TWENTY-ONE…"

Mother continued ranting as
I adjourned to our bedroom. I
shut the door and lay in bed.
Adrenaline coursed through me,
and I could hear the rush of blood
attempting to deafen my ears. I
felt nothing but fear that Mother
finally had enough and was going
to kill me and Dad. I could hear
her coddling Rody telling him
sweet nothings he doesn't damn
well deserve. I can only assume
they went to the kitchen because
the house fell silent.

I drifted to sleep. The sound
of Dad's car starting woke me up
at about ten o'clock. I didn't
stop him; I didn't try to wave
him down. I wonder what if I had,
would I be free from her sooner?

I could still be with Dad and not be so alone.

Blessings,

Willie

C. E. Brogan

Dear Roman,

Yes, she really did stab Dad. We have watched her humiliate and beat him many times. I don't understand how stabbing seems unbelievable. Mother is a cold-hearted woman. She hates us because she can't control us. We were always intelligent like Dad and she couldn't stand it. Writing more about her is just making me sick with resentment.

Do you at least understand my hesitancy about Mags? Why do I struggle to trust such a rushed affair? You've known her a few

short months, is that really
enough time to be talking about a
life together? Just be careful not
to kill rabbits until you're wed,
or risk being stuck like our dad.

So enough of that. I want to
speak more about my new life. Of
how accomplished I am becoming. I
AM MORE THAN THAT BITCHES SON!

I am quite enjoying living in the
barn's loft. The quiet is new and
so wonderful. I can experience my
thoughts more clearly. Marcus paid
an electrician to get electricity
up in the loft. I now have lights!
No longer do I have to end my
day at dusk or use a dangerous
oil lamp. Marcus said he did not
want another Chicago Fire here in
Cincinnati.

I've come to learn Marcus is quite a wealthy man. I guess his family's wealth survived the market crash. He pays me a whole dollar an hour for my work in the butcher shop. I assume it's partially for the free labor I give around the farm as well, I'm sure.

Next week we go to pick out a hog so I can try my hand at raising pigs. Marcus has a friend who raises them. The one we're probably purchasing is already nine months old, so I can spend the summer rearing him and getting him more comfortable with me before we start "whoring him out," as Marcus says.

I haven't decided on a name yet.

If you have ideas, you always
named our pets when we were
younger.

 Mother calls Marcus often to
check in on me. I refuse to speak
to her. That woman is out of my
life. I have had so much peace not
seeing Mother. The reminder of
her existence is irritating, but
Marcus is just too kind to ignore
the calls.

 Marcus and I get along for the
most part. His kindness confuses
me often, especially to the whores
who visit his butcher shop. He
shared that most of the men who
visit the shop also visit them.
That it's better to deal with them
for the business than lose their
clients who use the shop as an

excuse for their wives.

It's vile that we even partake
in the activities of adulterers.
There's not much I can do.
Marcus clarified that it was a
mote point, to discuss. It's
despicable, but I believe the
local police partake with these
sinful actions. It's ironic these
men uphold the laws for others but
them damn selves.

I continue to have interactions
with that pitiful nightwalker
"Candy". Marcus says it's because
she's taken a liking to me, but
knows better than to say I should
take her up on her devil's trade.
The whore likes to bait me into
arguments by calling me "The
Virgin" even though she rightly

knows my damn name.

"Candy" has become such a prevalent person in my waking hours her disgusting vibrant red hair has entered my dreams. It's tasteless, obviously dyed, and the ends look like they've been dipped in mud. She also must originally be a blond since she hasn't kept up with the color; you can see the golden strands creeping from her skull.

I wouldn't normally share these dark dreams but I hope you can help me decipher this one. I attempted to share my dreams with Marcus but he wasn't raised in the same dark hell we were. He doesn't understand why I'm plagued with these thoughts and thinks I should

consider a damn shrink. Mother
sent us plenty growing up. I know
what will happen and I don't have
time for it.

   You will have to suffice to get
these hauntings of my dreams out
of my head.

   After a fight with Candy-that
the whore should go to a church-
we returned to the farm and
had dinner. Marcus reprimanded
me for my lack of compassion,
he chastised me for my harsh
judgement instead of kindness and
understanding-that people make bad
choices in hard times. I couldn't
listen. Candy kept plaguing my
mind. I kept wondering what
she'd look like if her life was
different.

Possibly her short auburn hair
would be long kept in a braid.
Maybe she'd be married with
children coming in on Saturday
to pick out a Sunday roast. Or
maybe she'd have all her teeth and
visit the awkward butcher shop
apprentice many days in a row
because she was infatuated with
him.

I left the table with all these
thoughts in my head. Maybe Candy
could be those things she just
needed pushed in the direction.
Maybe she could transform for
the beast she is into a beauty.
Shaped into something magnificent.
She does have lovely birthing
hips and besides her teeth, she
is in shape. Underneath Candy's
revolting sinful lifestyle

are good genetics, with clear Norwegian ancestry in her features.

These thoughts continued through my mind as I drifted off to the realm of sleep.

I awoke to a kitchen similar to the ones in magazine advertisements. A petite auburn woman stood at the sink, washing dishes. Her scarlet hair twisted into a tight braid that fell just below the woman's shoulders. Humming cheek to cheek. I knew in my heart this woman was my wife.

I approached the tiny framed goddess from behind. I lay gentle kisses on the woman's neck. She smelt of sweet honeysuckle in the

July heat. Her skin was soft and dewy with sweat from the heated steam of the sink. Her words were the sweetest melody of love played by the recognizable instrument of Candy's voice.

Lulled into a siren song, she turned to me and I saw her face. A gentler younger Candy, one I have never had the pleasure of meeting. She pulled her hands from the boiling water of the sink. They were boiled, the flesh sloughing off the bones of what were the gentle fingers of a pianist. She pushed her melted hands through my hair, leaving a bit of flesh woven in each strand.

I smiled, and she smiled in return. As her rouge lips spread across her face, the gaping hole where Candy should have her front teeth emerged. I saw something wriggle in that darkness, that void in her teeth. She used her hands to pull me closer into a kiss. As I closed the gaps, I saw what was in her mouth. Fleshy, puss filled maggots writhing in her maw.

She spoke and they spatter into my face; the melody gone. A new instrument making its entrance into the score of the music of our love. Mother's slithering serpent's voice came out.

"You belong to me boy…" she hissed. I tried to pull away and the bones of her fingers gripped tighter, puncturing my scalp. I

screamed, but no noise came out.
This music didn't feature the
harmony of my fear.

The monster hissed "Willie,
Willie, WILLIE." Gripping me
tighter, pulling me towards
the mouth of this creature. It
unhinged its jaw like a snake. Its
face transformed into something
truly grotesque… Our mother.

I screamed and fought in
deafening silence. Until the
crunch of bone paralyzed me. The
sound of her bone fingers piercing
my skull. I couldn't fight. I was
frozen as she pulled me into her
maw.

I woke up in a sweat, with an
awful headache. As if the dream

poking its ugly little fucking
head into my reality. I felt like
vomiting. I showered for work and
scrubbed my skin raw.

   Will mother ever really loosen
her grip on me?

   Blessings,

      Willie

C. E. Brogan

Dear Roman,

Obviously, my dreams mean I have unresolved issues with Mother. It's not like I can resolve them with the bitch. If you have any actually useful ideas, that'd be lovely. No, I am not in love with some godless whore either. I just see the appeal that the sinful men who use her for the devil's work do. I do like the name choice for my new hog. "Wilhem" is very Nordic and not quite a "William Junior" but close.

I'm proud of you finally in your own place. Have you told Mother about this woman? That you are getting married? If not good on you, Mother would just ruin it. Are you sure though this person is the one? I really think you should contemplate this further. You haven't even introduced her to me. I understand not bringing her to Mother, but don't you trust me? The best decision I believe, would be to bring her here. I won't have a bias of "Love" to distract me in evaluating her. We will make plans for you to come here and bring her.

I bought Candy a bible. I will let you know how it goes. This woman can be crafted and molded into something better. I got one from the reverend at the Methodist church I've been attending with

Marcus. It's a quaint small church, quite liberal compared to the baptist church we attended with Dad.

  The Reverend is a nice man, never preaches on the atrocities of sin, he focuses on the glory of heaven. Which feels like he may lead his flock astray. What is the point of heaven if you don't face sin? Love is meaningless if it is freely given. Our God may be good, but he WILL bring wrath upon those who sin. If not by his hand, he will place people on this earth to rid it of such disgusting sinners. Which this reverend doesn't seem to understand.

  He is good enough now. I am not interested in spending the

sabbath hunting for a church that understands the truly horrifying depths of hell for those who sin. I also need to keep an eye on Marcus. I grow more and more concerned Marcus may be being led into a path of sin due to this pastor. His love for others is far too great not to be lulled into the world of sin. Marcus spends too much time with the monsters who lurk on the street peddling sin. He may think he is helping, but that's only for the devil to lull him into a false sense of security.

Marcus took me to pick out my hog. When we arrived at the farm, Marcus was uncomfortably friendly with the man we were buying from. He was a portly man, his teeth gnarled and rotten from ages of chewing tobacco. If I'm truthful, if we were at the local zoo, I'd assume he was an escaped ape with his disgusting layer of shoulder hair. Being within a foot of him, you could tell that bathing was not within his vocabulary. He smelt of putrid, dying animals, and feces.

The man introduced himself and put his hand out to shake mine. His hands were disgusting, missing his pinky finger, and the rest crusted with a layer of dirt. I had to muster all of my feigned kindness to return his gesture without vomiting. Marcus was kind to him. Even though he ranted at Marcus for not coming the day before on the Sabbath. WHAT DEVIL

WOULD WORK ON THE SABBATH! Marcus laughed it off even though it was CLEARLY AN INSULT TO OUR BELIEFS! I was livid. Marcus sensed my anger and waved me on to pick out my hog. I was happy to oblige and went on to the barn.

My face heated with fury as I opened the barn, the sickening smell twisted the fury to disgust. The smell of the animal's waste was vomit inducing. When I walked in, I saw over sixty hungry beastly hogs in a frenzy. Biting and snarling at each other. It's what I imagine the third circle of hell from Dante's inferno to look like. Monsters laying in their own filth and eating it as well as each other.

When I said pick out really I meant 'find'. Marcus had already picked a hog out and sent me to find him. I was given an idea of what the beast looked like. In the tornado of filthy animals fighting each other, I hunted for our beast. Marcus told me he'd be the only one with black skin. Apparently among its "litter", it was the only one that was back. The superstitious, ignorant farmer said he didn't want the beast and sold him to Marcus for a good price.

I saw no such hog in the frenzy. I heard a loud snarl, though, and the snapping jaws of the other hogs halted. The snarl rocked something deep in my soul. A stirring of fear and destiny as

a beast tripling the size of the
morbidly obese farmer appeared. It
truly had an ominous aura about it
that matched my own. The monster
looked closer to a wild boar than
a farm pig. With its twisted tusks
and deep black void for eyes. It
had blood running down those very
tusks, dripping upon its black
hide.

As the beast walked, it commanded
the gathering of the beasts, just
as Moses had done to save the Jews
parting the red sea. A younger
hog than the enormous beast walked
across its path towards the slop
in the trough. An apparently
unwise decision as the large
black hog snapped its hungry maw
onto the younger small pink hog's
shoulder. It left a large bleeding

bite wound as a warning, letting the younger know it could do much worse. I never knew hogs could show mercy.

Marcus eventually joined me, but I was too mesmerized by the grand ebony monster to know when he arrived. Marcus and the farmer exchanged some words and cash. I approached the pen and extended a hand to the magnificent beast.

"I wouldn't do that if I was you." The farmer said, spilling his tobacco out of his lip.

I ignored him, and his warning as the hog approached. He snorted and sniffed at my hand. He leaned his head forward in permission to scratch an itch he had.

"Hello, Wilhem…" I muttered under my breath. I knew as he responded in a pleased snort; we were one and the same. Two misunderstood monsters who didn't fit in anywhere.

At least Wilhem will get laid.

Blessings,

Willie

Dear Roman,

Wilhem is adjusting well. He is in the barn below my loft. I wake up each morning and feed him. I have found myself on the Sabbath, spending most of my time with Wilhem. He's a great listener. I've told him about Mother and Dad. How much of an idiotic cunt Roddy is. I swear he understands, or at least he snorts at the right timing.

Wilhem has grown quite a bit this month, We're looking for a good suitor for him. We've gone to multiple farms looking but have found not a single sow that is a good match. (According to Marcus). The hunt will continue.

 At the butcher shop, Marcus has allowed me to take over more responsibilities. He's been training me on how to butcher beef and make sausages. It's an amazing process, dissecting the muscle, removing organs, and he's allowed me to take a cowhide to make into a rug.

 Our most recent butcher was a pig. A fat, large, beast-not quite as big as Wilhem-but almost. Marcus hung the pig's lifeless hunk of a body from a hook with my help and the farmer who brought him in (The same fat farmer we purchased Wilhem from.) I grabbed a bucket and placed it under the hog. Marcus took his curved blade like an artist with a brush and slit the hog's arteries. The blood poured like a fountain sliding down its hanging body, painting it red. The blood produced a slight steam in the chill of the massive cold room. We stood and waited, listening to the waterfall of blood splash into the bucket.

Once the bucket was filled, Marcus moved to its bloody hide. He placed well aimed cuts along its tough skin. Soundless little jabs across its body. Marcus called for me and pointed at the cuts to dig my fingers in. I slid my fingers into the still warm carcass's skin. Each finger grasping both the inside of the skin and outside. He yelled for me to pull down, and I did just as he commanded. The sound of flesh separating from the hide was deafeningly loud. It sounds like when Mother would rip fabric while sewing. A long draw out tear that made my bones ache.

As the white membrane ripped between the body and the hide, I couldn't help but feel like I was opening a grand present. A piece of our Lord's artwork laid before me. The ripple of pink and white muscle cascaded in waves along the carcass. Each with purpose and meaning. Not only as our food, but an homage to the hog's strength. Layer upon layer of muscle is a cog in a machine of movement.

As I held the hide in my hand,
I saw Wilhem's bite mark scabbed
and scared on where the shoulder
of the pig was. I said nothing,
though. I don't want to ask the
farmer about why he chose this hog
among the many to bring here to
the slaughter. I will take it as
destiny that Wilhem will always be
with me now.

Marcus took the hide from me and
placed it in a to-go bag so the
farmer could turn it to leather.
The farmer accepted it and left.
Stating he wasn't interested in
what he considered the foulest
part of butchering his animal.
Marcus placed the knife in my
hand. He led me to the belly of
the white membraned carcass.
He placed his hand over mine,

whispering in my ear directions
of how to slide the knife. He
helped me puncture the beast. It
was cathartic as the knife slid
through the silver membrane down
the stomach muscles. Reminding
me of Easter when Dad left. How
his duty was to carve the ham,
becoming my life's work.

 The visceral organs slid out as
I drug my knife down. Slapping
across the concrete floor.
Splashing my shoes with remnants
of blood. Marcus had me pull the
wet, warm, organs still hanging
in the chest cavity. It felt like
Mother's jello disaster dinners
between my fingers. We keep the
intestines and other organs to
repurpose into sausage casings.
The feel of the organs made the

hair on my neck stand on end. It was thrilling.

Marcus shared that human and pig organs are very similar, or at least that's what his father told him. It piqued my interest in our own anatomy as a species. I have been visiting the Cincinnati Library to pick up books on the subject. How great our maker is to make the wonderful puzzle that is a human. The way each organ is placed perfectly in the abdomen is truly breathtaking.

When I left the Library, I saw Candy. Sitting on the steps reading. Who would guess a night walker could read? I chuckled a little to myself at the sight. I approached her and sat beside her. She was reading Alice in Wonderland. She was just as surprised to see me as I was to see her. In the daylight, she appeared so much prettier than at night. She was dressed in a turtleneck sweater and a long skirt. We spoke for a long time about life, and the places she'd been. A civil conversation, no arguing, just talking. Candy is so much more than I ever thought. I invited her back to the loft to continue the conversation, which I honestly don't remember. It was like someone else took over and wooed her. Something, someone better than me, much more clever than I.

I must lean on whoever that is, that was inside me. Is that what you do? Is that why you're so charming? Is it because it's not really you? Something I will need to reflect on if I'm to train Candy into a being better than the whore she behaves like.

Willie

C. E. Brogan

Dear Roman,

Mother has lost it. Rody has finally done it. She came banging on Marcus' door, demanding to speak to me. I originally refused and pretended to be asleep when Marcus brought her to the barn. But Mother doesn't take no for an answer. I'm shocked that with her weight, the ladder to the loft didn't break and kill her.

Marcus had turned the whole loft into a flat with a wall and a door that has a ladder that leads to the barn floor. I left it unlocked, which was damn moronic

of me. She came barreling through
the door like an elephant charging
at a field mouse.

"WHERE IS YOUR BROTHER? WHERE
IS MY RODY?" She snarled at me,
spewing her spit like venom.

I sprung up out of bed ready to
defend myself when shoes started
flying.

"What the hell are you talking
about, woman?" I hissed. My heart
was pounding. When I moved out
here, I cut her off. I haven't
seen her in almost a year. It was
like seeing a ghost. A really,
really fat ghost.

"WHERE IS MY SON! WHERE ARE YOU
KEEPING HIM?" Mother screamed like
a possessed walrus. She stomped to

the bed, causing an earthquake in the tiny loft.

 "Rody? Why the hell would I know, he lives with you." I could feel a deeper inner fire of rage being stoked within my chest.

 Of course, she would only come because of Rody. The moronic whore would never come to see her eldest child of her own accord. Mother got low, putting her face into mine. I could see every damn disgusting pockmark on her face. Her twisted, unkempt, filthy eyebrows were black; speckled with gray hair. Her grease ridden flee den of pepper gray hair tied up into a bun. I wanted to hit her, I just want to leave a mark like she had left so many on me.

"William." She said in a low voice. "Rody is gone, and he said he was staying with you in his letter." A growl came deep from within her as she pressed her nose against mine.

The pungent smell of alcohol singed my nose, "Why in the hell would he come here?" I hissed back, matching her intensity.

"Because, he wrote he was." She pulled her face back. Her rage turned to confusion painted across her face. She pulled a crumpled piece of paper from her dress coat. "I am going to stay with Will."

I laughed. I couldn't believe she stormed in, thinking Rody meant me. I tried and failed to sputter out a sentence "You... Ha... Thought... Hahahahaha"

"Stop laughing, idiot. Who else would he be talking about?" mother scowled, crossing her arms.

"Will Benings, his pen pal from California. He never once has called me 'Will'. I thought he was your favorite, yet you don't know about Will?" I raised an eyebrow. I was shocked, if I'm honest. Then it clicked. "Are you drinking again, Mother?"

She looked at me, completely defeated. As if she was a mother deer, watching her fawn be torn up by a wolf.

It took me back. I felt like a

small six-year-old boy. A Bucked
tooth with a lisp wearing trouser
two sizes too small After Rody
was born, when she fell into
Melancholia and lost Mom. The
moment when she became Mother. No
longer deserving the title that
doting moms get. When Rody was
born. I remember his yellow skin
from then, how sick and small he
was.

Tears ran down Mother's face.
"I have truly lost everything.
Haven't I, boy?" She collapsed to
her knees. "God doesn't forgive
sinners like me."

I could feel myself walking to
Mother. "Mom." It didn't sound
like me, though. As if a ghost
of the past was possessing and

controlling me. I kneeled and placed my arms around her. "It will be okay." I took a deep breath and exhaled. "Rody is an adult. He will be okay."

She grabbed my arm tight. "Promise." She muttered out. "So you will come home then." A rush of fear stopped my heart, as if the engine had stalled. I tried to pull away, but she wouldn't let go. Mother's nails dug into my wrists. I felt frozen watching the drips of blood roll off my arm. While it was mere moments, it felt like a milenia watching the drop of blood fall like a slow rain.

"No, I can't." I tugged my arm away, dragging her nails deeper into my skin. I was stuck in a

bear trap; the more I pulled,
the deeper her talons went into
my flesh. "Mom, please stop."
I wanted to yell, but my voice
trickled out in a whimper.

"You need to come home, you're
my boy, my first baby. I can't be
alone, Willie." Such loving words
were thrown at me in a hiss.

I pull free my arm, leaving
gashes from my wrist down my
hands. I backed away as she
stood. Her eyes turned from the
dull brown to a fiery amber. I
ran to the loft door and opened
it. I felt her claws dig into my
shoulders.

"YOU ARE MINE! I MADE YOU! GOD
WILL SEND YOU TO HELL FOR THIS!"

The banshees screamed, but all I could hear was the thumping of my heart. I froze as her hands began to travel around my neck...

I wrote this to you im real
something took control of me I
would never hurt anyone but the
frightened beast hidden deep in
my soul. I had no choice but she
began to wrap her fingers around
my neck. I had no choice. I had no
choice. GOD SHE GAVE ME NO FUCKING
CHOICE! FORGIVE ME ROMAN. FORGIVE
ME ROMAN FOR I HAVE SINNED! GO
SAVE MY SOUL OH GOD WHAT HAVE I
DONE I PUSHED HER DAMMIT I PUSHED
HER OH GOD OH GOD OH GOD FORGIVE
ME FORGIVE ME.

Mother left. I will no longer be in contact with her. Don't reach

out to her either; it's not worth
your time. I pray for Rody on his
new journey as you should as well.

   Blessings,

   Willie

Dear Roman,

I am beyond ecstatic to write to you today. I can't wait to tell you about my new project. I have taken it into my own hands to save our night walker who prowls behind the butcher shop. I have high hopes of saving Candy from her own sins. She is being saved from the hands of Satan. I have been praying hard for this and I think I've made a breakthrough.

For the past couple weeks, I have been working to break down the tension between Candy and I. I have greeted her cordially in the evenings when Marcus and I leave work. Marcus has also given me permission to give her some of the meat that doesn't sell and will go rancid soon. It is working fantastically. It reminds me of when we were trying to get that stray dog to like us. Luckily, Mother isn't around to scold me for leaving scraps again!

After a few days of that, she was excited to see me! I made so much progress so quickly. Then I moved on to encourage her to dress more modestly if she was going to be hanging out behind the butcher shop. Candy told Marcus and me that she didn't own more than a few modest pieces. Marcus told me I should be careful. I told him that God is calling me to save

her and to speak against this was
speaking against God. He shook
his head but hasn't questioned me
since.

Marcus keeps watching me, though,
when I speak to Candy. Possibly a
twinge of jealousy? When I talk to
her on my breaks, he always finds
a way to be outside with me. It
feels odd. I want to bring it up
to him, but I doubt it will make a
difference. I think I just need to
watch what I say around him.

I went and bought Candy more
modest clothes. When I gave them
to her, the light came back to her
eyes. She was so excited and gave
me the biggest smile I'd seen from
Candy. Then she tossed her arms
around me, and it took everything

in me not to throw her off. I know
she doesn't understand purity or
chastity. That will be something
we need to work on. Proper women
don't show affection like that in
public. It almost made my skin
crawl when I felt her hands on my
body. I quickly removed her from
me, but she didn't seem bothered
by the way my hands gripped her
wrist. She smiled widely at me as
I gripped her. It reminded me of
how she had so many missing teeth.
That's another fix for when I
have the money to buy her some new
teeth.

Brother, when you began to
court your women, did strange
feelings ever overtake you?
There was a moment standing in
the back with Candy where I felt

her body pressed against mine and a tightness formed low in my stomach. As soon as I removed her, I realized the arousal in my trousers. Whatever it is, it feels like a sin. I must pray tonight, ask God for forgiveness and strength; I refuse to turn into one of the men that Candy entertains. I know I am better than this urge. I hope in time, I can purify her of these urges as well.

I took Candace "Candy" to dinner the following night. She wore one of the dresses I purchased for her. It was a royal blue with light lavender embellishments. Even though I prayed before we met, my body again responded in sin at the

sight of her. Do you know how to
alleviate this stress? It makes
me sick to my stomach whenever it
stirs.

Candace and I walked down to the
river, and brother, you should
have seen the way her face lit
up when I escorted her onto the
massive Paddle Steamer. It wasn't
long after we boarded that the
massive wheel-shaped paddles
started to turn, and we were
sent to the top deck for drinks.
I was surprised at the rate at
which Candace downed her first
glass of wine. And when she asked
for another. I asked her to slow
down, promising her there would be
more to come after this. We stood
along the railing admiring the
Cincinnati skyline, and the sunset

painting the buildings in the same
colors as the autumn leaves.

   While Candace sipped her wine,
I studied her. Women should be
sturdily built, and also elegant.
Even though Candace has flaws,
like her teeth, and her profession
is one of sin; I have to admit she
can be quite lovely when she's
clean. I look forward to more
outings where I can woo her with
the charm I feel I am growing
into.

   Conversation flowed so easily.
The appetizer was a light salad
topped with deviled eggs. Candace
did not seem to understand the
etiquette of not talking while
you are chewing. I corrected her
once, explaining that if she must

speak before she has finished, she should hold a napkin over her mouth. However, she did not heed my advice. It seems as if we may have more work to do than I expected.

Candace was so interested in my job. Over dinner, I explained to her how to properly remove the knee bones in a lamb leg, and where exactly to cut between bones to separate the chops from the spine. She listened, nodding the entire time. By the time dessert was brought out, I was really starting to feel like we may build a connection.

The boat brought us back around nine o'clock. We walked a distance together before she went her own

way, back toward what I would
imagine was her home.

Hopefully, I will have more to
share soon.

Blessings,

Willie

C. E. Brogan

Dear Roman,

I was fooled. The Devil had me in his grasp and I thought it was the love of a stupid, useless whore. I hate her. I HATE HER! The things I did for her. I GAVE HER SO MUCH! I am an absolute idiot. God wasn't calling me. She was no Mary Magdalene to be saved but a Jezebel to lead me away.

I caught that moronic little slut performing fellatio on a poor man led astray.

Marcus and I stayed later at the shop longer than expected. We had

multiple animals to butcher. The
cold room was covered in viscera
and blood. One piece of cow's
intestines was frozen to the
floor. I had to take an ice pick
and break it off.

Each slam of the ice pick into
this solid piece of intestines
spattered tiny frozen pieces
across my face and clothing. It
was cathartic to methodically
pick away at it. Each stab made
this sickly crunch sound. Similar
to the sound of a spoon scooping
shaved ice. I kept picking and
picking and picking and picking.

I heard the beast snarling, and
calling me. I feel it in my bones.
An immeasurable ache to move.
To follow. My blood was on fire

although my skin was ice sparkled
with scarlet snowflakes.

   I was in a fog, deep, and
nothingness. I was not alone.
In the mist I saw the blackest
monstrous boar with horns in
front of me. His tusks were like
blades. The void of where its eyes
should've been had been blood and
puss seeping out of the gore.

   He led me through the fog, to
the back entrance. He charged the
metal door and it swung open. Then
suddenly I was on the other side
as the door slammed shut.

   It was cold outside, an autumn
wind blew through my hair, I could
feel her. Her betrayal. I felt
like the cow whose heart I had

ripped out in the cold room. I
watched, I watched her take him…
The disgusting, worthless slut. I
watched her. The heat was bubbling
inside. I felt wrong, but I
watched her until he finished.

 Candace's scarlet hair blew
ever so gently in the wind like a
flame. She was wearing the blue
wool sweat I bought her. Her pale
skin glowed in the light. I didn't
see the poor soul in Candy's
succubus snare. He didn't exist. I
put my hands in my pocket and felt
Dad's hand gun. Then nothing but
darkness.

She's mine. Mother Candy.. Mom
Candace.. Mike. All Mike only Mike.
MINE MINE MOTHER MINE LOATHE LOVE
HATE HER I WANT SHES MINE

MINE MINE MINE MINE MINE MINE MINE
MINE MINE MINE MINE MINE MINE MINE
MINE MINE MINE MINE MINE MINE MINE
MINE MINE MINE MINE MINE

I was filled with so much rage.
I wanted to peel my filthy skin
off. The way I felt was wrong. I
was blind with hatred. Next thing
I know, Marcus' hand was on my
shoulder. We loaded his truck and
went back to the farm.

Marcus knew, he knew something
was wrong. He looked at me like
Dad used to. When he knew Mother
had broken us.

"You'll be fine, boy? Remember
Deuteronomy 22:21." Marcus' voice,
deep and gravelly, shook me from
the empty void of my mind. "You're

a real mess. You better come to
the house and wash up."

I made a wallet recently. It's
to remind me of Mother. I made it
from leather I tanned myself. I
won't be speaking to her anymore,
but it doesn't mean I can't
remember the good times.

Remember when Mother took us
fishing at the Ohio river? I doubt
it since you were so young. Before
Mother picked up the drink. We sat
on a bank; the water moved ever so
slowly. I could see my reflection
in the water. Mother leaned over
holding onto you with father and
for a moment it was like a perfect
family portrait.

I killed my first fish that

day. I caught a huge bluegill.
Our family lost everything in
the Great Crash of 1929. That
bluegill meant we got to eat. I
can remember pulling in the foot
long fish. Dad cried, we had eaten
nothing at all that day besides
bread. It was one of the rare
times Mother said she was proud of
me.

   I am angry. I am angry she hated
me. Why didn't she want me?

She is mine.

   Willie

C. E. Brogan

Dear Roman,

I am fine, you shouldn't worry so much. I am ~~perf~~perfectly aware of my faculties. You say the beast is a sign of evil but it has only shown me good. More than God has ever shown me. Pray about it? Pray to whom? I have been pondering this for a while…

What has God done for us? We had a perfect home, and God took that away. We had an amazing father and now he's run from the monster God gave for us as a mother? He calls us to respect our parents. What parents beat their children? What

parent runs and leaves his eldest
son behind?

There is no God of love. He is
not our protector. Only one of
rage. He appears to me as the
beast. The beast is just, and
seeks justice for those wronged.
He is guiding me more in life than
any "good book" ever has. I don't
know Roman.

On a lighter note. Marcus has
finally promoted me! He has new
found confidence that I will
succeed independently. Today I
butchered a few lambs. Ironic
representation of "God" being cut
piece by piece.

When they brought the lambs
to the cold room, the hide had

already been removed. The lamb's meat is almost the same hue of Mothers favorite pink dress to wear to church on Sundays. First, I removed the viscera, saving the intestines for sausages and kidneys for deviled kidneys. When I pulled the kidneys and intestines, they had already cooled. The kidney felt like a gummy bear squeezing the mass in my palm.

I squeezed it until it finally popped the inside of the kidney oozed between my fingers like gelatin. I could spare one to satisfy my curiosity.

After I removed the viscera, I began work on hacking the lamb apart. I removed the neck first

by placing the knife through
the larynx and snapping the neck
bone. It cut like butter with the
new blade Marcus bought me for
a promotion. The hardest part
is sawing through the spine.
Sawing through bone will make you
perspirate-even in a cold room.

I butchered five lambs on my own
before my lunch break. Then I went
to lunch with Marcus to discuss
our breeding of Wilhem. I recently
brought a sow home. I decided to
name her Candy after that STUPID.
EVIL. VILE. SWINE OF A WHORE.
I'm keeping her in a pin next to
Wilhem's even though he continues
to tear and break through his.

Candy is gentle enough. When I
enter her pen, though, she lashes

out at me. When I tried to enter her pen this very morning to feed her, she bit me. Not too deep, but she drew blood from my forearm. I luckily had gauze and could do simple wound care. I don't want Marcus questioning my ability, so I will have to keep it covered. Luckily it's fall so I can wear a sweater.

Candy is quite the yeller. Which is why Marcus took me out to see if anything could be done about her noises. He was irrationally angry about her. There's not much I can do. Sows are just naturally louder than boars. I wonder if putting her in the pen with Wilhem will calm her nerves.

I don't notice her screaming in

the loft. I have been sleeping deeply. My dreams have swallowed me whole and sometimes haunt my waking hours. I feel like there's someone following me. I know it's just fatigue from not sleeping. Last night was one of the worst I've had in a long time.

At first, I didn't realize it was even a dream. I had laid down in my bed and heard a knock on my loft door. It sounded like yours. Remember how you always would knock three times, getting increasingly louder with each one.

Knock

Knock

KNOCK

I honestly was in shock. I thought to myself, it can't be? Did I miss a letter? There was a rush of joy. I lifted my arms and they wouldn't move. I was so tired from work that day. It must've been the weight of the wool. It took every bit of my strength to lift that blanket.

I felt drunk. I could barely stand. Everything was spinning before my eyes. The yellow and brown hues swirling around me. I collapsed. The blurry wool blanket strewn across the floor, my only marker to where I was.

I hadn't slept in three days. It only makes sense to blame it on exhaustion. I was so excited I had to keep moving forward. No matter

how much my body tried to stop me
from moving.

  I dug my hands into the old barn
floor and pulled myself forward.
Knee up, hand up, knee up, hand
up. As a child would to avoid the
thorn bush overhead. As I did when
hiding under Mother's roses.

  My grip began slipping as my
fingers trickled small dew drops
of blood. I hadn't even felt the
old rusted nails as I tried to
reach you. It felt like life or
death dragging along the floor. I
had a sense like bits of me were
being left behind as I drew nearer
to the door.

Knock

Kn●ck

KNOCK

I suddenly felt light. As if
I had left the bits of pieces
of myself that were weighing me
down. Keeping me back from my true
wants. I felt the c●ld of the
brass handle in my hand. It felt
like electricity shooting up my
bones. It was transcendent.

I twisted the knob and swung open
the door.

It wasn't you.

●r it was for a moment.

I watched your kind eyes morph
into cruelty. Your body swelled.

Then as your face turned to hers.
I heard a crack. Your neck, no,
Mother's neck snapped before my
eyes.

She began to weep bloody tears.
The blood dripped down her face,
across her nose. A drop splattered
the floor, and it sounded
like thunder. Mother took slow
footsteps towards me. I calmly
stood there as she approached.

I had to show her. That fear is
something I no longer feel. That
it was hanging from a nail on the
floor. She leaned into my ear and
whispered with a breath colder
than ice.

"You are just like me." Hissed
through my skull.

As she pulled away, her skin turned into an ebony hide. Her face elongated. I looked into the glossy red eyes of the beast. In the reflection of bright red hair which had been dipped in mud. Then as the cloven hoof shoved me I fell into the abyss below I heard a gun fire.

Don't give me the 'I need to see someone' lecture. I am fine. Marcus is just overworking me. I should probably take a day off to rest.

Willie

C. E. Brogan

Dear Roman,

You can tell Mags not to be scared. I am not a fucking madman. I have nightmares every so often, that's it. If she's "terrified" then why the hell are you two inviting me to stay with you? "To get help" that I don't even need? DREAMS ARE DREAMS, DAMNIT! Why is she sneaking through your mail? I'm not an invalid. I know you would never betray my trust by showing her. All women are too GOD DAMN NOSEY.

Congratulations on your wedding. I appreciate the invite but I

won't be joining you. I can't, nor
do I want to. Large parties make
me feel sick. I have never been to
one, but the thought makes me feel
ill. Being packed into a ballroom
with strangers I've never met
sounds horrifying.

I know that sounds crazy since
I work in a shop which has new
customers often. That's different.
It's only a few patrons at a time
and by this point I know most
of them. There is one man who
comes every Thursday at three in
the afternoon for ground beef
and bacon. He's a funny fellow,
always nagging about his wife. I
am really coming to the conclusion
women are not worth the trouble.

HA.

I sold him some of the meat
I actually cut. I am so proud
of myself and the progress I'm
making here. I am now considered a
butcher and not just an apprentice
now. Which often means Marcus is
not here. I feel now that he's
promoted me; he comes and goes as
he pleases.

I wonder whether it's trust that
I will run the shop or laziness?
As if he promoted me solely so he
could profit without working. What
could he even be doing? What could
a man with no wife and children
be up to in his free time? Just
sitting alone at home. He must be
up to something, but it's not my
problem.

I'm busy reading on how to get

the two pigs acclimated to each
other. Wilhem has been trying to
break the pin between the two of
them. I think it's frightening
Candy. She is about to go into
heat and she should be excited.
Instead, she cowers in the corner
away from Wilhem.

I tried releasing them into the
field for a bit, but Candy refused
to leave the pin as long as Wilhem
was out. It's like she is just
refusing to do what she is FUCKING
HERE FOR.

Wilhem has been a darling,
though. I read to him sometimes.
Don't laugh, from my understanding
pigs are highly intelligent
creatures. It's also quite nice to
feel needed.

Wilhem is quite aggressive towards Marcus. Just yesterday since Marcus was off I asked him to feed Wilhem. I warned Marcus to go slow and be calm. But did he listen? Of course not, I had to close up shop and take him to get stitches.

When I showed up at the farm, he had a sizeable chunk of his forearm missing. His white tank top looked like one of those avant garde "pollock" paintings. The scarlet adorning the white cotton was beautiful. If it wasn't so "morbid" I'd encourage him to keep it and put it in a frame and sell it.

If he had let me take the day off, then it would've never

happened. Serves him right.

I find it curious that for being
a farmer Marcus doesn't do well
with animals. Animals sense more
about people than we do. Marcus
has been quite fidgety lately. I
won't worry about it though. I'm
sure Wilhem is just picking up
the fear that Marcus has for him.
Right?

Wilhem isn't scared of me, nor
I of him. We have some sort of
unspoken connection. While his
ebony hyde is beautiful and would
make some nice leather, I think
I will keep him past breeding.
Marcus thinks we should butcher
Wilhem after. I told Marcus we
should butcher him instead, HA!

Marcus has been a little agitated with my refusal to come to church. Saying that a broken heart doesn't mean I should turn away from God. It's not just a broken heart, though. It's everything together. I know the God he worships is not a God of love. A God of love doesn't send you people to love you who are incapable of it.

I worship a better God. A God who sees my pain and eases it. Who has numbed me to heartache so I may never hurt again? The beast is patient. It takes my rage and holds it. It feeds the rage and grows it into something beautiful. Cathartic almost. Whenever it appears in my dreams, I feel at ease with the anger the next day.

It fuels me. The rage pushes me
forward. I am no longer ashamed
of it like God wants me to be.
No longer does shame and sadness
consume me. Only the joy from
accepting that a burning fire
inside me is a light to lead me,
not something that needs to be put
out.

I will be thinking of you during
your nuptials. Please send me
photos.

Willie

Dear Roman,

I fucked up; I fucked up so badly. Wilhem ripped Candy apart while I was watching. I couldn't help but stand watching the train wreck before me.

It was a cold night. I came home from the shop physically exhausted. I came back and Candy was still cowering in the corner. Her refusal to cohabitate with Wilhem has been so frustrating to me. I thought to myself fuck her. Fuck her refusal. I was angry and done with trying to acclimate them to each other.

I broke down the pin walls
between them. Wilhem had already
done plenty of damage, so all
it took was one good kick. The
cracking of the wood underneath my
strength gave me so much power.
Wilhem watched on as I did this.
Observing his master's will.
Taking on that aura surrounding me
into his.

I stepped over the small wooden
wall towards Candy. I think she
could sense my rage as she pressed
herself as hard as she could
against the pen wall. Shaking
in terror. I felt as though I
was underwater, consumed head
to toe, in a heavy, languid
substance. Time slowed down around
me. Consumed with rage, I was
unable to feel the full weight

of her trepidation and fear like
I normally can. My lungs burned
as though filled with water, and
my only focus was to relieve the
burning ache. As I approached,
watching her face morph into
a hopeless fear. I knew I was
grinning from ear to ear. Glad to
know I'd finally be done.

  That my mission would be
accomplished. She would bear the
piglets and nurse them. Then I
could cook her up. That the sow in
front of me would do her job and
be done.

  Wilhem approached her slowly. I
was positive things were going to
go well. His massive black frame
moved past me like a midnight
mist over the water. Possibly a

storm causing massive waves around
me. Stirring the muddy waters
below. He was slow and deliberate
in his actions, and I waited
patiently for him to smell out
his new companion. For the first
time in days, Candy was quiet,
pressed into a corner, wheezing. I
expected her to accept her fate,
and become complacent once she
realized she had no other choice.

As he placed his nose against
her, though, she let go of a
strangled cry. The sound pierced
through the stillness. She must
have frightened Wilhem; for as
soon as the sound left her, he was
upon her. He thrashed wildly as he
attacked. His great maw wrapped
around her shoulder.

Everything came into startling clarity as her cries began again. This time tinged with pain as he ripped away her flesh, exposing the muscle. He stepped down on her, and I heard a sickening crunch as he held her in place; tearing more pieces away from her, blood oozing from his jaws.

I felt frozen, but not in fear. I felt while this hadn't gone according to plan that I was in control. That this wasn't a bad thing. Relief fell upon me as I watched his body and the surrounding space turn bloody. I could just get another sow. One that would take Wilhem as he is. Not fucking reject him. Not destroy his fucking self-confidence every day.

I could hear the sound of Candy's screams reverberating around the barn long after she'ed stopped fighting. They continue long after Wilhem seems sated. I watched on as he pulled her viscera from her body. Playing with it like a cat with a field mouse.

Then I remembered where I was. That Marcus had invested in this, in me. Here she was dead, torn in so many pieces. I panicked. Marcus would be furious. I panicked.

So I bagged her up. Each of her pieces into a large plastic bag. All of her was still warm-slipping through my fingers like freshly cooked pasta. The plastic steamed from the heat.

It was amazing how much blood was everywhere. It all had to go. I had to come up with a plan to tell Marcus. I decided I would tell him she broke her leg. That she could no longer mate. That I put her down humanely. I'm sure he'd agree it'd be better to put her down than call for help.

I stared at the pen. How the fuck do I hide this part of it? I felt panic for the first time since the entire ordeal started. But then it dawned on me. The wall between the two pens was already broken. What if I just smashed through the gate to Wilhem's pen and let him run free? I could tell Marcus that he destroyed the pens in a fit of rage. I laughed openly at my genius. Wilhem could run through the field and down to the creek.

 Once, when he was smaller, he
squeezed through a gap in the
fencing, taking off toward the
muddy expanse of grass that
precedes the little creek running
through the property. By the time
I found him, he was so covered in
dirt and mud, I couldn't tell him
from the rocks he played around.
The blood and gore dripping
from him now would be washed
away, and anything left would be
unidentifiable.

 I can say someone left the gate
open. Since Marcus was supposed to
be the last one taking care of the
fields, he will willingly accept
the blame. I can say Candy tripped
on stones at the river and fell.

It was brilliant. I just had to
dispose of Candy's body.

I loaded her into the truck and
drove to the butcher shop in the
middle of the night.

Once we got there, I cleaned
her meat. I felt terrible rinsing
the shit and straw from the hunks
of flesh. Once she was cleaned,
I loaded her into the grinder
and started the process to make
bratwurst.

I saved a piece of her. An ear
to dry and remember not to unleash
Wilhem.

I am writing this before I speak
to Marcus.

Wish me luck he is not too angry
with me.

Willie

Dear Roman,

I will never be forgotten. I will no longer be under anyone's thumb. The beast has prophesied the future into my dreams. I have spent a lifetime bending to the whims of others. That is a truly forgettable life. True death comes from being forgotten.

No one has ever truly loved me beside the beast. The prophecy he wrote into the dreamscape of my sleeping hours is glorious, and I can't sit idly by and not share the future with you. It will cause you heart ache but it must happen or I will die.

  As I drifted off to sleep, I
became very aware of the sound
of my bed side clock ticking. A
metronome calling me forward to a
song I've never heard. I shut my
eyes for a moment but the ticking
got louder but yet sounded further
away. I stood from my bed. My feet
landed on the creaky old barn
floor. I couldn't hear the usual
creaks over the ticking echoing
outside of my bedroom door.

  Each step I took, electricity
thundered through my bones. My
ears rang as I felt warm liquid
fall onto my shoulders from them.
A migraine rattling my brain.

  I felt better the closer I got

to the door. The tension in my
muscles eased, and the migraine
lifted. I felt lighter and
lighter. Revitalized per se.

I grabbed the doorknob again
in the previous dream. I felt
trepidation at first. Fear of the
monster on the other side. I went
to pull my hand away and dad's
voice came through the door.

"Do not fear, boy. You are my
son, my true son, and heir to the
history I offer to bestow upon
you." I felt an instant peace over
me as I pulled open that door.

On the other side was something
I had never seen before. It was an
old study. As I stepped through,
the warmth of the old cobblestone

fireplace filled me. The crackle
of the flame matching the ticks
of the clock. Drowning it out. In
front of the flame, across the
bergburgundy carpet, was a large
leather chair with a high back and
brass-clawed feet.

Every book you could imagine
lined the walls of this study.
From the past and the future.
Endless knowledge lined these
walls and I could feel the history
speaking to me.

"Come closer, boy, join me
by the hearth." A tender, kind
voice called me. It sounded like
Father's, but with more strength
and confidence.

I moved forward not by force but

by choice. I never have control
of my dreams, but here I moved
willingly. I sat down on the floor
next to the chair.

  When I looked upon the man in
dad's old black funeral suit I
knew. I knew I was in the presence
of the truest form of the beast.
Upon the old suit sat a bear's
head, Wilhem's head. Not torn from
him, but a part of the beast.
Two beautiful ebony rams' horns
protruded from his head, almost
like a crown. The beast's eyes
were rubies inset in his sockets.
Looking upon his beauty was truly
comforting.

  "My boy, I have been waiting
for you. To share my knowledge.
To guide your future. You will

no longer be under the thumb of a piase false god or any other being. Look upon the flame, boy."

I gazed upon the flickering fire before me. I watched as phantoms of those who have wronged me screamed in silence, forming and morphing in the flames. First flashed Marcus, pained and confused as he morphed into Rody burning alongside Mrs. Lester.

"These people are nothing but mere humans." The beast growled.

Rody and Mrs. Lester combined into Doc, burning and tearing away at his own face.

"They will be eaten by time."

Doc shredded his face in the

flame to reveal Dad sobbing in pain. Dad wiped away his tears and his flesh along with it.

Candy appears cowering and fearful. She began screaming into the flame. I can't hear her, all I can hear is the crackling timed to the ticks of the clock.

"You have a choice to make. You can be forgotten and swallowed by the flames of time. Or you, my son, can live forever known by all."

Candy's screams turned from fear to rage. She bloated in her rage, fattening her up into Mother. I flinched hearing Mother's threats, degrading remarks and manipulation ring in my mind.

"Do not fear. They will all burn up. Forgotten and worthless. All people who have held you back through morality and oppression. You thought you had found a friend, but he uses you. A brother who could do no wrong getting away with what you were taught was sin. A man who tried to manipulate you to love him. A father who abandoned you to the wolves. Then the women you loved more than anything else, who rejected you. None of them will be remembered, only you, boy. Those mere beings do not deserve to be remembered and ilk like them shouldn't be allowed to walk this plane of existence"

I looked at the beast as a child would an elder telling a story.

"You follow your deepest, darkest desires and you will live on in history forever."

All I did was nod, confirming that I understood.

"Now go boy."

I stood to return to my bed, and he left me with a warning.

"Do not trust Marcus and his false God."

It brought so much clarity. The dream is a prophecy to do as I wish, feed my urges and I will be rewarded. That the beast, Wilhem and I are one. That only I will live on after death.

I had my suspicions of Marcus but
this solidifies it.

Willie

Dear Roman,

I'm sorry if I alarmed you with my last letter. I meant it as encouragement. I have found my purpose in life, it is an overwhelming relief to know that my pain hasn't been p●intless. Everything I have done has led me to this point.

I also #p##appreciate the lovely picture you sent of yourself on your wedding day. Your wife is just as I imagined a stunning woman of nordic descent. Dad would be proud of your choice.

I also have exciting news!
Marcus allowed me to make my own
bratwurst this weekend before the
Reds game. I had a recipe I wanted
to try, and after some convincing,
he finally let me make them! I
took the intestines from the lambs
we butchered and filled them with
a mix of Candy's pork and other
leftover bits from other animals.
Then Marcus let me sell them and
keep half of the profit. Every
single bratwurst sold! We had none
left at the end of the day, Marcus
couldn't believe it!

I was shocked at all the
customers and people we saw. I
ended up in a fight with this
one disgusting woman because she
dropped her first one. I politely
told her no, that I just had too

many customers to give one for free. That fat pig was just like Mother and screamed at me when she didn't get what she fucking wanted. "Scrawny boy!" she yelled at me. "You are just a stingy thief." I started to yell back, but then I remembered. She is just a mere human and will be forgotten. I flatly told her no and sent all the hatred I had towards her. My response to her seemed to scare her. I'm unsure why, but I think The Beast sent her away.

Marcus was upset I wouldn't just give her a new bratwurst. I reminded Marcus we are a business, not a damn charity. His business has garnered vastly more profits since when he's not there, I run

it like a fucking business. Marcus
is always droning on that he runs
a business to keep himself busy,
not become a millionaire. I told
him if you want to keep busy, pick
up a damn hobby. He just laughed
and said someday I'll understand.
I think someday he will be
forgotten as a useless old man.

Marcus seems to be aware I
know he can't be trusted. He has
been fidgety around me recently.
Marcus avoids me as well. When
I confronted him about it, he
claimed I've been more aggressive
as of late. Which is just a gas
because I have never felt more
calm or at peace with my life.
He constantly is spouting verses
and singing hymns while working.
Something that while I was blind,

I enjoyed, but now that I see it grates at my nerves.

"When will you join me at church again?" is all I ever hear from him. I can only take so much of his nagging, but I will not fall to him and his false God. His existence is beginning to drag on me. Marcus also refuses to care for Wilhem when he's at the farm. Saying that Wilhem is possessed by something. He wants to put Wilhem down but told me it's my pig my decision.

I sat with Wilhem and spoke to him about the situation. Wilhem says The Beast wants me to wait. The Beast wishes me to no longer be a virgin-before we can join my spirit to his and Wilhems. The

idea of waiting till marriage is
that of a false god. True power
comes from liberation and I can
not be truly liberated until I
have broken all the "sins" that
tie me down.

I was uncertain how to go about
this. I do not exactly have the
abilities of Casanova. Wilhem
reminded me though that love is a
concept made up by the false God
to hold us back. That if I was not
held down by the disillusionment
of love, I would have troves of
heirs. While women can only bear
one child at a time, I can plant
the seeds for an army.

I am learning so much from
The Beast and Wilhem. That all
the rules and morality that are

taught now are only to oppress
us. I should look to the pagans of
the past for true liberation. I
need to make sacrifices and live
my life freely to become truly
powerful.

Heed my warning. Change is
coming, a grand metamorphosis
of society. The Beast will take
his place in this world where he
belongs. I am the catalyst for
this change. When I find true
liberation from my inhibitions the
world will be released from its
prison of morality.

I will be named the pope of
freedom though they will call me a
monster. But hear me when I say I
am not. I will be a God. That the
ties that hold me to this plane

are meaningless. I will be free to
do as I wish and take as I want.

   I have enclosed a gift. A wallet
that I made earlier this year
to remind me of Mother; hold on
to it for me. I will let go of
this possession because I will
make more items and a new wallet.
I no longer have needs for the
reminders of the larvae I was as I
cocoon to become a new being.

   Willie

Dear Roman,

I am not crazy. I DO NOT NEED
HELP! I HAVE BEEN SAVED BY THE
BEAST! I AM NOT SOME DERANGED
MORON! I feel as though I have
been called by the beast to warn
you of what's to come. You are
just blind. It is no fault of your
own. You and your wife were born
with your eyes closed and taught
to keep them shut. You will be
forgotten if you do not OPEN THEM!
The Beast is the freedom to exist
without consequences. He will
not choose you unless you choose
him. Let go of your false sight
and your false sympathies. Align

yourself with others' nightmares, ascend into power with me. The mortal world, and the mortal people you call your friends and family, are merely distractions from the false god. I dream of your deliverance.

My dreams bring me to a higher power! You call them nightmares, but they are prophecies! An entire nation follows a book filled with prophetic dreamers but I AM THE ONE TO BE SCOFFED AT?? EVERYONE MOCKS ME AND NOW YOU DO AS WELL!! Roman, I implore you, consider my words before it's too late. For even now I suffer the hands of unbelievers, just as your false God's profits have. Do you not see that? Woe is the man who ignores the call of true sight. Do not

remain in your ignorance; it will
be your downfall.

  You will understand. You all
will understand someday. I do not
fault you for your confusion. I
am not angry with you. I am angry
that my brother is stuck in old
ways that will never serve him. I
must relinquish the idea you will
understand immediately.

  War is coming, Wilhem told me.
I suggest you prepare accordingly
at your age you will be called. I
will not be. Wilhem told me.

  I am beginning my next stages.
I finally am free of the label of
virgin. Wilhem told me how the
night walkers are like priestesses
of liberation. Preforming

ritualistic sex acts, freeing men from morals.

After work, I waited outside the butcher shop for nightfall and started to walk in the direction I know most of the prostitutes place themselves. I watched to pick the woman who will release me from the chains that hold me to this world's morality.

A few women approached, but none of them were right. Wilhem told me a specific woman would show herself to me. Only she could begin my journey to being known by the world.

I was walking down Longworth Street when I spotted her. She had long, beautiful, curly chestnut hair. Her skin was deep olive under the warm glow of the street lamp she was leaning on. Her skin was stunning; she couldn't have been more than twenty.

As I approached, I felt myself step out of my body and allowed The Beast to guide me. I could never have the courage or smoothness to charm a woman. I watched from behind my eyes as The Beast wooed her. Her laugh was contagious and like a song.

She introduced herself as Maggie. What a beautiful name for a stunning creature. The Beast shared the woes of being a virgin due to religion and realizing that's no way to live. She smiled and said, "Well first time is free

then, but only cause I'm counting
this as Charity."

Wilhem was right, they really are
priestesses working towards our
cause_willing and ready. We took
her back to the butcher shop. I
wasn't comfortable with performing
the ritual outside. The Beast
understood and shared someday I
would be freed from the fear as
well.

Feeling her under me was like
complete control. I was pure
power; an embodiment of true
masculinity. I understand now that
it was never about love. It was
always about power. A man's power
is strengthened by the complete
domination of a woman, and this
priestess of darkness fed into me.

She became the conduit of energy that brought me closer to the beast. I could feel his approval as he watched me atone for my confirmation to society. He gently reminded me of who I was meant to be. It was a fuck you to Mother who never thought I'd be doomed to celibacy! This power filled me, and I was released. Then, I don't remember much. I allowed the beast to return her to her post so I could rest. Next, I knew Marcus was banging on the loft door.

Marcus is becoming too suspicious of me. Wilhem sees Marcus climbing into the loft and looking through my things. I saw him wearing my sweater, so I know it is the truth. I have no doubts that he is planning to have me leave. I

plan on beating him to the punch
and leaving for elsewhere. I'm not
sure where yet.

I know he's having me followed by
his friends. I can not live under
his oppression. He was a stepping
stone to freedom, and I will
always be grateful for that. I
know he is watching my every move.
I can not allow him to interfere
in my grandiose future.

I told Marcus it was time. Time
to slaughter Wilhem, that we
should have a big party and roast
him on the spit whole. Marcus
thinks it's a wonderful idea. I
just want to respect Wilhem's last
wishes at the final ceremony to
release me from this form. I will
become free from my ties to here.

Ascending beyond the mere humans
at this celebration.

I will be free finally.

Willie

C. E. Brogan

Roman,

I am free. Yesterday we butchered Wilhem. Not once did Wilhem protest as he was led to the slaughter. He is a conduit, after all, the last piece of my transformation. As I slit his throat, I felt his soul swathe my body in red power before it seeped into my flesh and merged with my being. I can feel him in my blood, I can see with his eyes, I know his thoughts even better than I know my own. Greatness is close.

I have decided to move. I know I talk about it in quite a few letters, but I think I will actually go. My new residence is still a mystery to me. The beast has promised that he will direct my steps as long as I trust him and my intuition. When the beast comes to me in dreams now, he says we must go North first. He said there are people I must convert and others that I must smite for their deceptive, piased actions.

You have no reason to be alarmed, brother. I am invincible. No mortal can touch me. There is nothing to fear, for I have ascended to my highest purpose. Wilhem, the beast, and I are one and the same. Father, Son, and Spirit. My purpose is apparent now, my life is full. We will see each other soon, I promise. Once

I have fulfilled my true purpose,
I will come to you in glory. Fame
will follow close behind, and the
world will immortalize me. Then I
will shower truth upon you, and
your eyes will be opened to every
sin you have not committed, and I
will give you strength to submit
to the power in disengaging from
morality. We will live eternally
together.

When I settle, I will write
again.

With all my deepest affections,

Wilhem

Cincinnati Morning Inquisitor

Oct. 1, 1994

LETTERS SURFACE IDENTIFYING OHIO TORSO KILLER-MASS MURDERER RENAMED MIDWEST MONSTER

In June, a call was made to Cincinnati police regarding some suspicious letters a man found while cleaning out his grandfather's attic. The man wishes to remain anonymous but has allowed the story to be told. The letters were from his grandfather's brother, William (the last name is redacted for the family's privacy), during the years 1937-1939. The Cincinnati man turned in the letters when he learned of a cold case murder from 5 years ago that sounded similar. A total of 43 letters were submitted, along with the boxes they were kept in. Investigators were able to pull DNA from the man and matched it to DNA pulled from beneath the deceased's fingernails. This then lead to the identification of 5 unsolved murders and missing persons cases over forty years cold. Candace (Candy) Green, Margaret (Maggie) Brown, Grace MacArthur, Natalia Ancovick, and Maggie Parker; all prostitutes living in Cincinnati during those years. Each woman was reported missing days after their suspected disappearance, and only the torso of one body has been identified. Police still have yet to find the rest of the bodies. During the initial search of the boxes the letters came in, they discovered a suspicious wallet; after DNA and forensic testing, they believed it to be made from the skin of a human, possibly related to the killer. Sources claim it's made from the skin of the killer's mother, who also disappeared during the summer of 1938.

During the process, the Cincinnati police were contacted by investigators from Athens, Greenville, and Parma, Ohio. All investigators reported similar disappearances in the years following the murders in Cincinnati. After more forensic and DNA testing, it was confirmed that at least seventy percent of the victims had trace amounts of the killer's DNA.

The following month, police got a surprise call from Indiana investigators. They had heard of the unsolved murder cases in Ohio and believed the killer had lived in Indiana following his potential stint in Greenville. The case officially became a federal investigation in September when Kentucky and West Virginia requested samples of the letters along with DNA. West Virginia wanted to test the handwriting to see if it was a match for a slew of letters found buried with various body parts during a spree killing in 1974. They stated that 19 women went missing between April 1974 and December of the same year. While only 11 bodies or parts of bodies were recovered, they now suspect that the same killer may have returned in 1981 and is responsible for another set of 7 murders that had originally been thought to be associated with the nomadic Christ Family cult that plagued the US during the same year. Sources now believe that the torso killer is responsible for 119 murders and counting. One of William's earlier letters is quoted as saying, "Fame will follow close behind, and the world will immortalize me." Whether it was a true prophecy or the ramblings of a sick man–we will never know. The Midwest Monster has been named the world's most prolific killer, proving that William spoke the truth when he claimed his fame.

ELWOOD JONES-TRIAL UPDATE

The Ohio man still pleads not guilty even after the new evidence brought to light a few weeks ago. Jones is accused of the murder of a 67-year-old woman in the Blue Ash Hotel earlier this year. Investigators found fingerprints on a small-